BEST BIRTHDAY EVER!

By Christy Webster

Illustrated by Tommy Stubbs

Random House New York

Thomas the Tank Engine & Friends™

CREATED BY BRITT ALLCROFT

Based on The Railway Series by The Reverend W Awdry.
© 2020 Gullane (Thomas) LLC.
Thomas the Tank Engine & Friends and Thomas & Friends are trademarks of Gullane (Thomas) Limited. © HIT Entertainment Limited.
HIT and the HIT logo are trademarks of HIT Entertainment Limited. All rights reserved. Published in the United States by Random House
Children's Books, a division of Penguin Random House LLC, 1745 Broadway, New York, NY 10019, and in Canada by Penguin Random House
Canada Limited, Toronto. Random House and the colophon are registered trademarks of Penguin Random House LLC.
ISBN 978-1-5247-1651-6
rhcbooks.com
www.thomasandfriends.com
MANUFACTURED IN CHINA
10 9 8 7 6 5 4 3 2 1

It was a very special day on the Island of Sodor. It was Thomas' birthday!

Thomas' friends couldn't wait to celebrate. They each had a very special delivery to make for the big birthday party.

Percy was coupled with a flatbed so he could pick up the cake.

Rebecca was hooked up to two coaches so she could pick up the party guests.

Emily was joined with one flatbed and one coach
so she could pick up the band and their instruments.

But when the Station Master arrived, he looked very confused. "I'm sorry, engines," he said. "I've lost my schedule for today. One of you is supposed to go to the docks, one to Knapford, and one to the castle. But I don't remember who needs to go where."

The engines decided to split up and try their best. They wanted Thomas to have the best birthday ever!

Percy went to Knapford first. "Is the cake here?" he
asked the Porters.

"There's no cake here!" said a man. "We're the band!"
He tooted his horn happily. "Can you give us a ride to
the party, Percy?"

Percy didn't have any coaches, only a flatbed. "I can
take your instruments," he said.

Percy chugged away with the instruments.
He wondered if he would have time to pick up
the cake. Suddenly, Harold flew by.

"Harold, can you help?" Percy asked. "I'm
supposed to pick up a cake for Thomas, but I
don't know where it is! It must be at the docks
or the castle."

"I'll do my best!" Harold said. He wanted
Thomas to have the best birthday ever.

Train Conductor Race

Things you'll need:
Two hats • Two bandannas • Whistle • Two boxes • Tickets
(Use the cards in this book as tickets.)

★ Divide players into two teams. Have them form two lines behind a starting line at one end of the room. Give each team a conductor's hat and a bandanna, and give each player a ticket. Across the room from each line, there should be an empty box with a slot on top, labeled "Ticket Box."

★ Blow a whistle to start the race. The first player on each team must put on the hat and bandanna and run to their ticket box to drop their ticket into the slot. Then they must run back to their team, remove the hat and bandanna, and give them to the next player.

★ The first team to have all their tickets in their box wins the race!

Meanwhile, Rebecca arrived at the castle, hoping to find the party guests. But she only saw the baker.

"This cake needs to get to Thomas' party!" the baker cried. "Percy is late!"

Rebecca only had coaches. She wasn't sure how to carry the cake.

Just then, Harold arrived. "I'll take the cake!" he said. "I think Percy needs help at Knapford with the band." Rebecca hurried away.

Emily found the party guests waiting at the docks.
"Get these guests to the party!" Cranky said.
"But I only have one coach," Emily said. "I can
take half." Half the guests quickly climbed on.

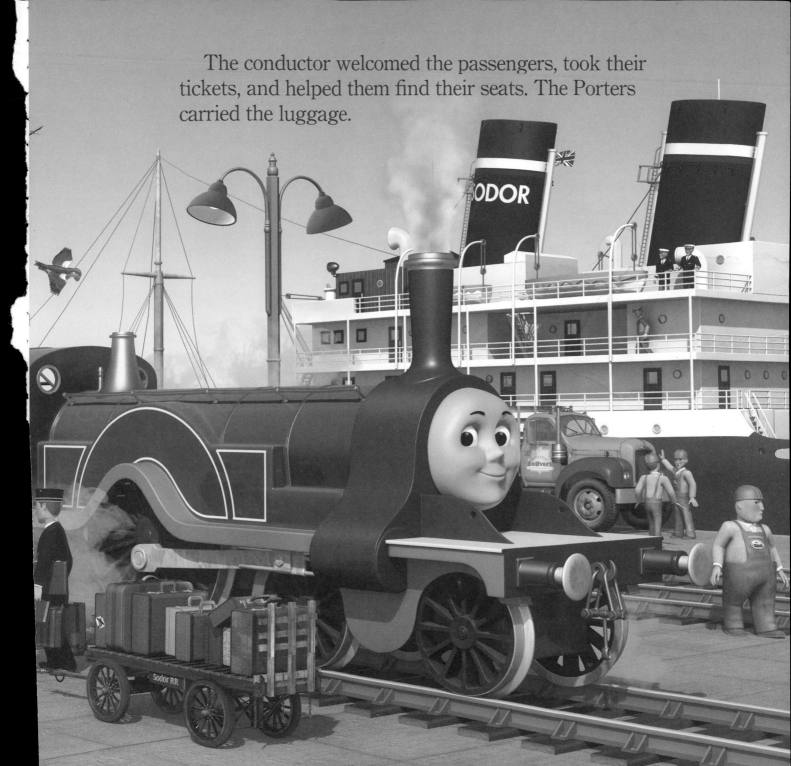

The conductor welcomed the passengers, took their tickets, and helped them find their seats. The Porters carried the luggage.

All the engines hurried as fast as they could with their cargo. They wanted Thomas to have the best birthday ever.

Pin the Party Hat on Thomas

★ Hang the poster on the wall.

★ Punch out the hat piece from this book, and give it to the first player.

★ A grown-up should give a piece of tape to the player whose turn it is (to secure the hat to the poster) and tie a handkerchief over the player's eyes as a blindfold.

★ Have the grown-up guide the player toward the poster, being careful not to let them run into anything.

★ The player should try pinning the hat on Thomas.

★ The person who pins the hat closest to Thomas' head wins!

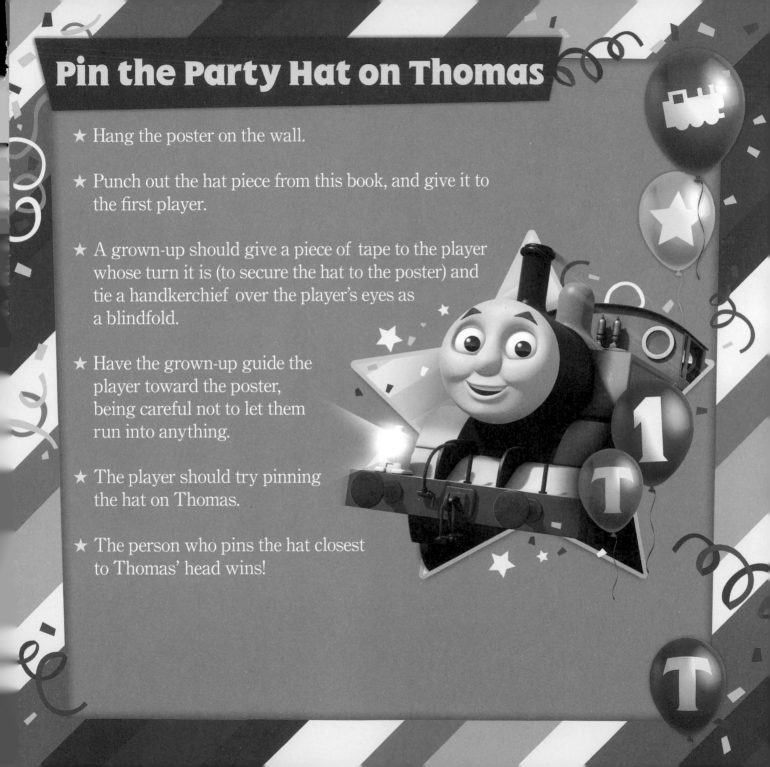

When the engines arrived at the party, they
saw the Station Master there.
"What are we missing?" he asked.
"The band is here," said Rebecca.

"I've got the instruments," peeped Percy. "And here comes Harold with the cake!"

"I've got some of the guests," added Emily. "Oh, no! The rest of the guests!" Half of them were still at the docks, waiting to be picked up!

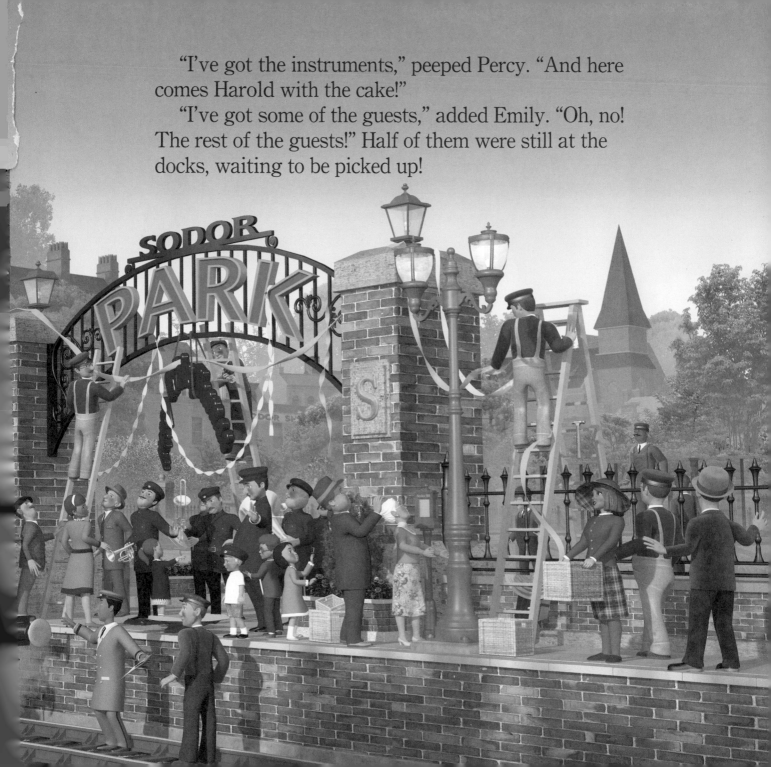

All three engines raced back to the docks. They wanted to be sure that all of Thomas' guests would make it to the party. Time was running out!

But when they arrived at the docks, they only saw balloons—hundreds of balloons!

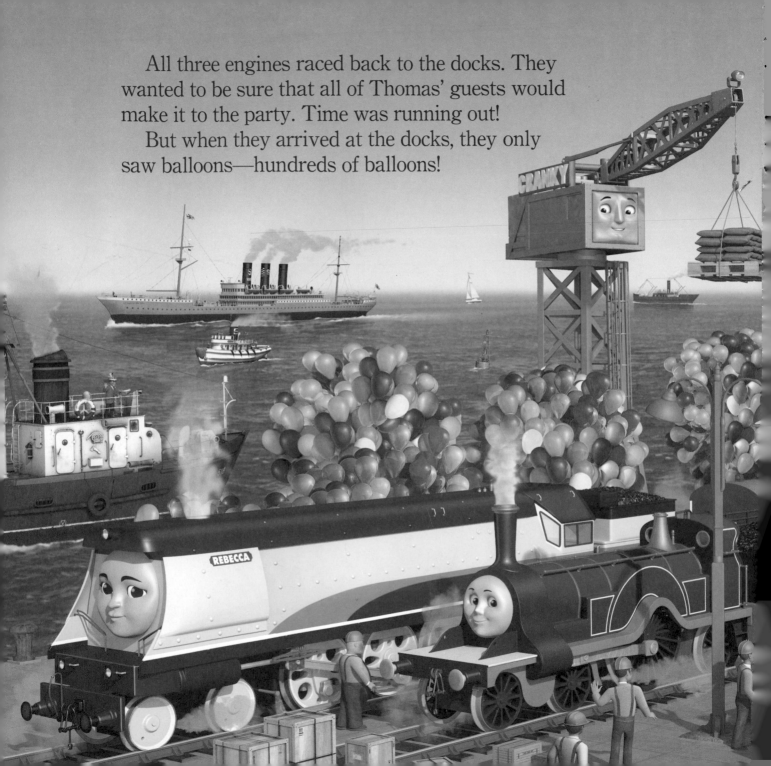

"The guests are already on their way," Cranky said. "But here—take these presents and as many of these balloons as you can. They are a surprise for Thomas. Hurry!"

The engines hurried back to the party, with their
coaches and flatbeds overflowing with balloons.
When they arrived, they were the ones to be
surprised. There was Thomas—with the other guests!

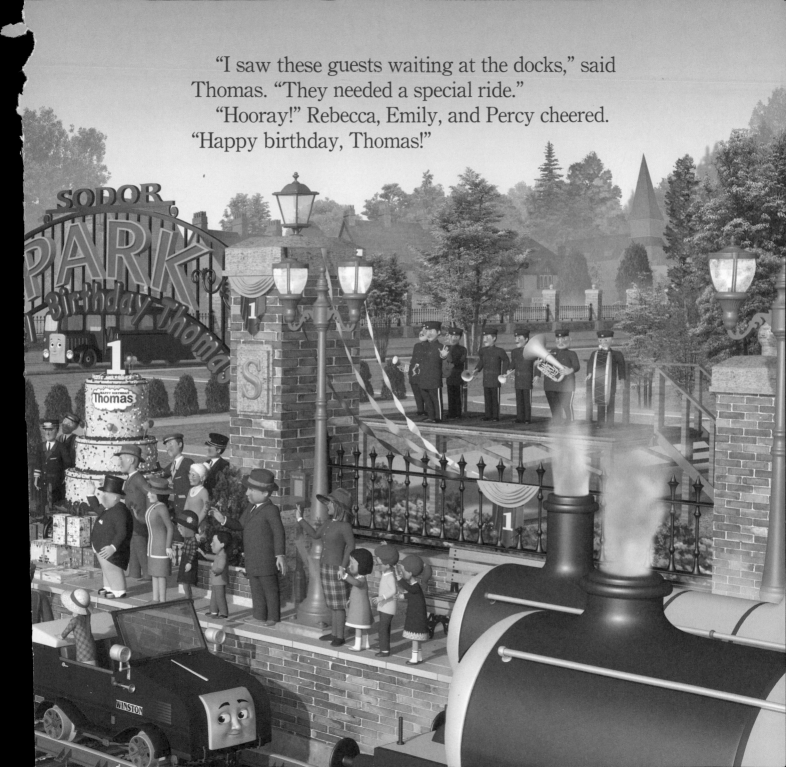

"I saw these guests waiting at the docks," said Thomas. "They needed a special ride."

"Hooray!" Rebecca, Emily, and Percy cheered. "Happy birthday, Thomas!"

Thomas loved the balloons. He loved the cake. He loved the band. He loved the whole party! He didn't know the engines had such a mixed-up day. Thomas only knew it was the best birthday ever.